THE HOUSE ON THE MOUNTAIN

THE HOUSE ON

illustrated by Leo Carty

THE MOUNTAIN

by ELEANOR CLYMER

E. P. Dutton & Co., Inc. New York

Published simultaneously in Canada by Clarke,
Irwin & Company Limited, Toronto and Vancouver
SBN: 0-525-32365-1
Library of Congress Catalog Card Number: 75-133123

Designed by Hilda Scott
Printed in the U.S.A.
First Edition

Other Books by Eleanor Clymer

The Big Pile of Dirt
My Brother Stevie
The Second Greatest Invention
We Lived in the Almont

This is something that happened on the Fourth of July. You know what that stands for. Liberty, Freedom, and all the rest. I don't know what this proves, but it must prove something.

I am a boy ten years old, my name is Joe Hulett. I live with my mother, my sister Gloria (thirteen), my little sister Beedee, and my little brother Frank. My father doesn't live with us. My mother works, and sometimes I'll go to the store and carry groceries for a lady and she'll give me a quarter. My sister Gloria is supposed to take care of the kids after school, but most of the time she doesn't. She is real lazy, or else she doesn't care. Or she's hacking around with these friends of hers. Sometimes I come home and Beedee and Frank are playing in the street, nobody watching them. I make them go upstairs and play in the house.

But it's not too safe there, they could play with matches.

I tell Gloria, Why don't you watch the kids?

She says, Why don't you leave me alone?

Because she's older, and thinks I shouldn't be telling her things. Sometimes I watch them myself, but not too often.

My mother worries a lot. She is always saying, This terrible neighborhood. She worries about Gloria. This crowd Gloria goes with, they smoke and do other things, and Mama isn't there to watch her. So Gloria says, What's the matter with the neighborhood? I like it, there's always something going on. I bet if you were my age you'd like it too.

So Mama says, When I was your age I lived in a better place.

And Gloria says, Yes, I know, without any bathroom.

And Mama says, There are some things more important than bathrooms. And then she'll start to tell about this place where she grew up. She has told it so often I could tell it in my sleep, and Gloria too, but the little kids will sit there with their mouths open and take it all in, especially Beedee.

Beedee is a devil, she never sits still a minute, and Mama worries about her too, I mean about what she'll do when she gets bigger. But when Mama starts telling about the house, she'll sit quiet and listen.

It seems they had a house on a mountain someplace in the south. There were woods all around, and they had chickens and a cow and a cat. The cat would have kittens sometimes. Frankie always liked to hear about the cat and kittens.

The house was little and old and had no paint, but was all gray from the weather, and inside there was an old black stove that they cooked on, and two rooms and an attic where the kids slept, and outside was a barn for the cow, and a well where they got their water, and a little house that was the toilet. It sure must have been cold to go there in winter.

And they had a garden with vegetables, and flowers growing in tin cans on the porch.

And Mama would get up early and feed the chickens and eat breakfast, and then run down the mountain to school. And that's where she met Pop. He went to the same school.

And they didn't have to wear shoes, but went barefoot, and waded in the brook and picked berries and

nuts in the woods. The more she told the better it sounded.

One time I said, If it was so great why did you ever leave there?

So Mama said that when she was old enough she and Pop got married and had Gloria, and Pop couldn't make a living, so they came to the city. Then they had the rest of us, and then Pop left, and this is where we are now. And Mama works and we get welfare, and sometimes Uncle Art helps us.

Uncle Art is our father's brother and he lives near us. He and his wife have two kids of their own, but still they help us out sometimes. We go to their house and Aunt Lily sends stuff home, ham or a pie or something she made, and sometimes they give us clothes and Uncle Art bought us a TV set. I say to myself, when I'm older I'll get me a job and make enough so Uncle Art doesn't have to help us. I'll be a ball player and be interviewed on TV and make a pile of money and Mama won't have to worry anymore.

I don't talk about it, because I once did and Mama said, Don't you go fooling yourself with those crazy notions. That's what happened to your father, he had big ideas, too big. You just be like your uncle.

My uncle is a floor polisher. His boss has these machines, and he goes around to different buildings where they are painting, or to new buildings, and he scrapes the floors and puts shellac and wax on them and polishes them.

Sometimes I go over to their house around supper time, when Uncle Art has just come home from work, with dust from the floors all over him. He'll wash up and eat his supper and then he'll tell about the places where he has been working, fancy apartments downtown somewhere.

Once my aunt said, Stop talking about such places, the kids will just get discontented listening to you.

Uncle Art said, Why shouldn't they hear about other places?

Aunt Lily said, Why don't you bring those machines in here and polish our floors? They could stand it.

Uncle Art said, If I brought those machines in here they'd go right through the floor. (That's the kind of house they live in, and ours is about the same.)

Well, one day when I was there, with the little kids (I had to mind them, that day), Uncle Art came home and told Aunt Lily, The boss asked me to go to his house in the country on the weekend and do the floors.

Aunt Lily said, He did! And where is that?

Uncle Art said, Oh, up the river someplace.

She said, How are you going to get there? And he said that the boss would let him take the truck.

So my aunt said, Is he going to pay you extra? Uncle Art said no.

Aunt Lily said, He should if you're working on your own time. You should get time and a half. That's union pay.

Uncle Art said, Well, the boss asked me as a favor and I couldn't say no.

She asked, When are you going? And he said, The Fourth of July.

I was listening, and when I heard that I said, The Fourth of July? Oh, no!

Uncle Art looked at me surprised and said, What's the matter?

Well, the thing was, I was hoping we'd go to the beach. But Mama had to work on the Fourth. The lady she works for was going to have a party. So Mama told me and Gloria we had to stay home with the kids. But Aunt Lily told Mama, Don't worry, because we are sure to go somewhere and we will take your kids along, so they won't have to hang around the street on the Fourth. And now Uncle Art had to work too.

I sat there feeling as if it wasn't fair, and then I had an idea. I said, Uncle Art, could we go with you?

He and Aunt Lily looked at each other, surprised, and then Aunt Lily said, Why not? After all, you're doing him a favor.

Uncle Art said, You want to go?

But Aunt Lily said, No, I hate the country.

He said, Well, I can't do my work and mind six kids.

I said, Gloria and I will mind the kids. (I thought that would be better than staying home.)

So he said, I guess it would be all right. There won't be anybody there. Okay, if you and Gloria keep them out of my way.

So on the Fourth of July we went. Gloria didn't want to go, she and Mama had a big argument, but finally she gave in. My aunt packed a lunch and we all got in the truck. Uncle Art and Gloria were in front, and the rest of us were in back with the machines, me and the kids and my cousins Allie and Danny.

It was fun. We looked around at all the houses we passed, and yelled at people, and at last we got to the boss's house.

It was a new development. There was a lake with boats on it, and all these new houses, just for summer. Some houses weren't all finished yet. There were boards and bricks lying around. Some were finished and there were people in them. The boss's house was not quite finished, so nobody was in it. There was no furniture yet, that's why he wanted Uncle Art to do the floors.

It was a nice day, the sun was shining. Uncle Art got ready to work. He got his machines off the truck and into the house. He said to us, All right, now you can play.

I looked around for Gloria. She was sitting by herself under a tree.

So I thought, Well, Uncle Art brought us, I guess I have to play with the kids. I had my bat and ball, and I got them started playing ball on the lawn in front of the house.

But Uncle Art came out and said, No! Not on the grass, it was just planted.

So we played in the cement driveway. It was awfully hot.

We could see the lake from where we were. It was shining in the sun, and there were people swimming, and other people in boats. I thought, If we could go in the water we could cool off. But Uncle Art had not told us to bring our bathing suits.

So I said, Okay, kids, let's take off our shoes and we'll just wade in the water. So we went down to the lake.

The water was nice, so cool and clean, not like the river where I sometimes go swimming.

Gloria went off by herself and sat on the end of a boat that was pulled up on the sand. She just sat there looking off into the distance, as if she was dreaming. She was no help.

That left me in charge. Danny and Allie started to play in the sand. They were no trouble. And Frankie wouldn't have been any trouble, but Beedee gets him all excited. She's always starting things. The first thing I knew, she was taking off her clothes, right down to her underpants. Thank goodness she didn't take those off. And then Frankie took his clothes off, and then they were both running into the water, splashing and laughing like crazy. And when Danny and Allie saw them they did it too.

You couldn't blame them. A bunch of little kids, and some nice clean water, it was natural.

Then a lady came out of a house nearby and came over to us and said, Where are you children from?

I said, From the city.

She said, I thought you didn't belong around here. You can't swim in the lake unless you have tags. Now go away at once.

So I had to make the kids come out of the water and put their clothes on, and we went back to the boss's house.

Uncle Art was just coming out.

I said, Are you finished?

He said, No, I just stopped for lunch. Where were you kids? Why are you all wet?

I said, The little kids were playing in the water.

He said, I forgot to tell you, you can't go in the water.

We sat down in the shade of the house and opened the lunch. It was good. There was chicken and potato salad and cake. Uncle Art ate fast and went back inside. He still had a lot of work to do.

But we were thirsty. There wasn't enough to drink, just a few bottles of soda. So the kids started to fight.

Allie said, I want a whole bottle. Danny grabbed it away from him.

Gloria didn't do anything. She just sat. I said, Why don't you do something? She said, What is there to do?

But Beedee found something to do. She started looking around, and in back of the house she found a hose. And before I could stop her, she turned it on and was drinking out of it, and Frankie and the rest came to get some too, and she sprayed them and they all got wet.

I yelled at them to stop, and then Danny found a tree with little green apples on it. It was a good tree for climbing. So in a minute he was up in the tree throwing apples down at the rest of us, and I was yelling at him to come down, when another lady came out from a house. She looked real worried.

She said, What are you children doing here? You don't live here, do you?

I said, No, ma'am.

She said, Well, why are you here?

I said, My uncle is working here, polishing the floors.

She looked relieved and said, Oh. All right. But don't make so much noise.

And she went back to her house. Another woman

23

came out and I heard her say, Did you find out anything? The first one said, It's all right, they're not moving in. The man is just working here, and I guess he brought his children with him. I only hope they don't do any damage.

I thought, What am I going to do with those kids? It was getting hotter all the time. I could see other people in their yards, or down by the water, having fun, cooking lunch on their barbecues, playing ball. There was nothing for us to do. I started to wonder, How did I get myself into this?

I looked around, and across the road there were trees. It looked cool there. I said, Let's go over there. (I was thinking to myself, If any of you kids start anything, I'll sock you. I almost wished they would.)

So we all went across the road. Gloria came too. It was cool under the trees. Then we saw that there was a hill. There was a road going up the hill, under the trees, a dirt road with grass growing in the middle.

I said, Let's go up there and see what's at the top. (It was just something to do till Uncle Art got through working.)

Gloria said, I don't want to climb that old hill.

I was getting sick of her doing nothing. I said,

24

Come on, you better help with the kids or I'll tell Mama. She said, Who cares? But she came. We started up the road.

It was nice in the woods. The trees grew up high and made a kind of ceiling, and you could see pieces of the sky between the leaves. It smelled good. There were flowers growing, and Allie picked some. I didn't see what harm it could do. He likes flowers, and they were just growing wild.

It was cool, and there was a brook that ran down the hill beside the road. I guess it ran into the lake. The kids took off their sneakers and waded in the brook, climbing over the rocks. They had some kind of green moss on them and it felt soft but slippery. A couple of times we sat down in the water. Danny caught a frog. But it got away.

It was a good idea to go into the woods. For about the first time that day I was glad I came.

Then we got nearly to the top, and suddenly we came out of the trees, and we were in a sunny open place, and in the middle of it was a house.

It was a little house. It was gray, and had a little porch, and on the porch were some flowerpots with red flowers in them. There was a rocking chair with

a cushion in it. And in front of the house was a garden with other flowers, all colors.

There was a barn.

It was very quiet. We didn't see anybody. But then, around the corner of the house came a couple of chickens. They were saying cluck, cluck as they walked, as if they were talking to themselves.

We stood there looking, and I was about to say, Okay, kids, let's go, when suddenly Beedee let out a scream.

I said, What the heck is the matter with you? And she yelled, It's Mama's house!

I thought she had gone crazy. I said, What do you mean, Mama's house?

She said, It is! It is!

Then I saw what she meant. It did look like what Mama had been telling us about, a litttle house on a mountain, with a barn and flowers and some chickens.

And suddenly Gloria, who hadn't said a thing, said, It's for real!

I saw what she meant too. She had been listening to Mama all this time, and she thought Mama was just making it all up. She didn't really think there was such a place because she couldn't picture it.

And here it was!

Danny and Allie didn't know what we were talking about, but Danny started trying to catch one of the chickens, and Allie began picking flowers. I said, Hey, cut that out! Because those weren't wild flowers. Somebody had planted them.

I looked around for Frankie, and he was walking toward the barn. A black and white cat was there in the doorway. Frankie loves cats. He sat down in the dirt and the cat walked right over to him and he patted it.

Then I turned around and saw what Beedee was doing. She walked right up on the porch and opened the door.

I said, Hey, What are you doing?

She said, I'm going in. It's Mama's house, isn't it?

Then I understood. She didn't just mean it *looked* like Mama's house. She meant it *was* Mama's house. All this time she knew there was a house but she didn't know where it was, and now she had found it! And of course she was going in.

I jumped up on the porch after her and grabbed her, but she had already opened the door and was walking in. So I called out, Anybody home? Just in

case somebody was there and might see the door opening and start throwing things, or in case they had a dog. But of course there couldn't be a dog or it would have started barking by then. But there was no answer. Whoever lived there had gone away and left the door unlocked. Probably they never thought anybody would come in.

I thought, We ought to get out of here. But I couldn't help it, I was curious myself. So I went in too.

There was a black iron stove, and a table with a red cloth on it, and shelves with blue dishes. There was a sink with a pump in it instead of faucets, and a couch by the windows, and white curtains. There was a bookshelf with books, and a couple of rocking chairs, and some lamps but no electric wires. They were kerosene lamps. Mama had told us about them.

On the table was a plate with doughnuts, covered with a napkin. Beedee marched over and helped herself to one. So then all the other kids, who had crowded in behind me, went and took some too.

I said, Hey! Stop that! What do you think you're doing?

Beedee said, Why not? Mama wouldn't mind.

I said, Beedee, that's enough. You know well and good this isn't Mama's house.

She said, It is so. I can tell. Look, there's the other room with the bed in it, and there's the attic.

It's true there was a bedroom, and there was a ladder going up to the floor above.

I said, It isn't, Beedee, it just looks a little bit like it. Mama's house was far away from here.

She said, It's on a mountain, just like this.

I looked around for Gloria. I thought, Maybe she can talk some sense into this kid. But Gloria was just standing there with this far-off look in her eyes. I thought, Maybe she's on a trip somewhere, she sure doesn't seem to be with it. What's wrong with every-body?

And just then I heard something. A car. It was coming closer and then it stopped. And a dog barked.

I thought, What will I do now? We'll get arrested and Uncle Art won't even know where we are!

Just then the dog rushed in, barking like crazy, jumping around, showing its teeth, and the kids began to scream and try to get away, and a woman screamed, and a man's voice hollered, What's going on here? Who are you?

I tried to answer him, but the dog was barking so loud, and the kids crying and screaming so, I couldn't yell loud enough for him to hear me. So at last he got hold of the dog and put him outside and then he said, Okay, now explain. And it better be good.

All I wanted was to get out of there, and I said, It was just a mistake, mister, we didn't hurt anything, we were just taking a walk and there was this house and we just wanted to see if anybody was home—

But the man wasn't buying that. He said, Don't you know better than to walk into someone's house?

I said, We didn't touch anything.

But the woman said, What about those doughnuts? How do I know you didn't take something else? I said we should lock the door. You can't even come to the country for a weekend—even out here isn't safe from these—(She said a word I wouldn't repeat.)

And then something happened. My sister Gloria woke up. She pushed everybody aside and walked over to Beedee and took her hand.

She said, We apologize. My little sister loved your house so much she wanted to see it. It looks just like the house we used to have long ago. But I see it isn't like that house. Ours was a nice house. Good-bye.

And she marched out, pushing Beedee ahead of her, and all of us following. And we all started walking down the hill. **1592218**

Going back, Beedee sniffed and held on to Gloria's hand but she didn't cry anymore, and the other kids didn't either, they just hurried along. It was getting late. The sun's rays were slanting through the trees, and suddenly Gloria said, That's how it used to be in the mountains when it was getting near sunset. It was nice then.

I said, How do you know? And she said, I remembered.

I thought, How can she remember, she was only two when they left there.

But I didn't want to argue with her and maybe start the kids crying again.

We got back to the boss's house and Uncle Art was just putting his stuff back in the truck. He said, Where in the heck were you kids? I was just going to look for you.

I said, Oh, we went in the woods and climbed up the mountain.

I was hoping Danny and Allie wouldn't start tell-

ing about going into the house, at least not right away. I didn't want Uncle Art to start bawling us out and have them cry and have to listen to them all the way home.

But they didn't say anything. We all climbed into the back of the truck, Gloria too. We were all pretty tired. We lay down on some quilts that Aunt Lily had sent along, and Uncle Art started. Frankie and Allie and Danny fell asleep. I leaned against the side of the truck. The sky was getting dark blue and the stars came out. The evening air smelled cool and nice.

We were riding along, first through the dark country, and then past houses with lights in them, and car lights flashed past us, and my head was nodding. Frankie was asleep across my lap, and I was almost asleep myself, when I heard Gloria talking. She had her arms around Beedee and she was talking to her in a quiet voice.

She was saying, No, that was not Mama's house. But Mama's house is somewhere else, and someday we will go there, and Papa will come home, and we will have a cow, and work in the garden, and Frankie will have a cat, and you'll go to school, and I'll stay home and clean the house. And Mama will be home

too, she won't go out, and we'll have chickens, and you will feed them and get the eggs—

And she went on and on, till I wanted to say to her, Why don't you quit telling that kid all those stories?

But she kept on, and pretty soon I was almost believing it myself. I could see the house and the chickens and the cat and the garden, just like the place we had seen that afternoon.

And I started to tell myself stories. I thought, I'll always remember that little house in the sunshine on top of the hill. And when I'm big and have a good job as a ball player, I'll go back there and buy it, and I'll buy a car and take the whole bunch there and they'll say, Joe! Did you do this?

I guess I fell asleep then, because the next thing I knew, the truck had stopped and we were in front of our house. Mama was lifting the kids out and saying, Did you have a nice Fourth of July? And I thought, Oh, yes, this was supposed to be the Fourth of July. And I heard Gloria saying, So long, Uncle Art, thanks for taking us.

ELEANOR CLYMER calls *The House on the Mountain* "a story of contrasts. Now that I live in a small, quiet village, I find myself writing about places and people I knew when I lived in New York City, and the contrast between their life styles. In a small village, one is much more involved with and aware of the comings and goings of people.

"The story is fictional, but the idea arose from a visit by a large family of children to a vacant house next door to the one where I once stayed. I wondered how the neighbors would welcome such a noisy, happy family, and how the children would react. The story grew from there. The house on the mountain is one I discovered when I was climbing by myself, years ago in another place." Mrs. Clymer's other books for children include *We Lived in the Almont*, *My Brother Stevie*, and *The Big Pile of Dirt*.

LEO CARTY has found time, along with illustrating children's books, to teach a course on black art at Fordham University and to continue as president of Anton Studios, a black greeting card company he founded.

Mr. Carty prepared his art in stages. "First the illustration is drawn on board in pen and ink. A wash is then applied to establish the darks and lights and to soften the edges. A felt-tipped pen is used to accentuate some of the line drawing under the wash. Finally, white paint is used to cut back the wash in some places and to accent the light areas." Mr. Carty's other recently illustrated books include *Nat Turner* and *Where Does the Day Go?*

The display type is Caslon Antique and the text type is Janson. The book is printed by offset.